Dedalus Euro Shorts
General Editor: Mike Mitchell

Dedalus Euro Shorts is a new series. Short European fiction which can be read from cover to cover on Euro Star or on a short flight.

Mercedes Deambrosis

An Afternoon with Rock Hudson

Translated by Mike Mitchell

Dedalus

Dedalus would like to thank the French Embassy in London and the Institut Français du Royaume Uni for including An Afternoon with Rock Hudson in the Burgess programme of the French Ministry of Foreign Affairs and the Centre for Books of the French Ministry of Culture for its assistance in producing this book.

Published in the UK by Dedalus Ltd, Langford Lodge,
St Judith's Lane, Sawtry, Cambs, PE28 5XE
email: info@dedalusbooks.com
www.dedalusbooks.com

ISBN 1 903517 35 4

Dedalus is distributed in the United States by SCB Distributors,
15608 South New Century Drive, Gardena, California 90248
email: info@scbdistributors.com   web site: www.scbdistributors.com

Dedalus is distributed in Australia & New Zealand by Peribo Pty Ltd,
58 Beaumont Road, Mount Kuring-gai N.S.W. 2080
email: peribo@bigpond.com

Dedalus is distributed in Canada by Disticor Direct-Book Division,
695 Westney Road South, Suite 14 Ajax, Ontario, LI6 6M9
web site: www.disticordirect.com

First published by Dedalus in 2005

Un Apres-Midi avec Rock Hudson © *Editions Buchet Chastel 2001*
Translation © *Mike Mitchell 2005*

The right of Mercedes Deambrosis to be identified as the author and Mike Mitchell to be identified as the translator of this work has been asserted by them in accordance with the Copyright, Designs and Patent Acts, 1988.

Printed in Finland by WS Bookwell
Typeset by RefineCatch Limited, Bungay, Suffolk

This book is sold subject to the condition that it shall not, by way of trade or otherwise, be lent, resold, hired out, or otherwise circulated without the publisher's prior consent in any form of binding or cover other than that in which it is published and without a similar condition including this condition being imposed on the subsequent purchaser.

A C.I.P. listing for this book is available on request.

THE AUTHOR

Of Spanish and Greek origin, Mercedes Deambrosis is a new and individual voice in French fiction. *Milagrosa*, her first novel,(Dedalus edition 2002), has been described as a revelation, a stylistic tour de force. Marie-Claire said, "Mercedes Deambrosis is an unknown. That is quite normal, this is her first novel. But what assurance! One would swear it was written by an author at the height of her powers."

An Afternoon with Rock Hudson is Mercedes Deambrosis's second novel.

THE TRANSLATOR

Mike Mitchell is one of Dedalus's editorial directors and is responsible for the Dedalus translation programme. His publications include *The Dedalus Book of Austrian Fantasy*, *Peter Hacks: Drama for a Socialist Society* and *Austria* in the World Bibliographical Series. His translation of Rosendorfer's *Letters Back to Ancient China* won the 1998 Schlegel-Tieck Translation Prize after having been shortlisted in previous years for his translations of *Stephanie* by Herbert Rosendorfer and *The Golem* by Gustav Meyrink. His translation of *Simplicissimus* was shortlisted for The Weidenfeld Translation Prize in 1999 and *The Other Side* by Alfred

Kubin in 2000. He has translated the following books for Dedalus from German: five novels by Gustav Meyrink, three novels by Johann Grimmelshausen, three novels by Herbert Rosendorfer, two novels by Hermann Ungar, *The Great Bagarozy* by Helmut Krausser, *The Road to Darkness* by Paul Leppin, and *The Other Side* by Alfred Kubin. From French he has translated for Dedalus two novels by Mercedes Deambrosis and *Bruges-la-Morte* by Georges Rodenbach.

institut français

French Literature from Dedalus

French Language Literature in translation is an important part of Dedalus's list, with French being the language *par excellence* of literary fantasy.

The Land of Darkness – Daniel Arsand £8.99
Séraphita – Balzac £6.99
The Quest of the Absolute – Balzac £6.99
The Experience of the Night – Marcel Béalu £8.99
Episodes of Vathek – Beckford £6.99
The Devil in Love – Jacques Cazotte £5.99
Les Diaboliques – Barbey D'Aurevilly £7.99
Milagrosa – Mercedes Deambrosis £8.99
An Afternoon with Rock Hudson – Mercedes Deambrosis £6.99
The Man in Flames – Serge Filippini £10.99
Spirite (and Coffee Pot) – Théophile Gautier £6.99
Angels of Perversity – Rémy de Gourmont £6.99
The Book of Nights – Sylvie Germain £8.99
The Book of Tobias – Sylvie Germain £7.99
Night of Amber – Sylvie Germain £8.99
Days of Anger – Sylvie Germain £8.99
The Medusa Child – Sylvie Germain £8.99
The Weeping Woman – Sylvie Germain £6.99
Infinite Possibilities – Sylvie Germain £8.99
Invitation to a Journey – Sylvie Germain £7.99
The Song of False Lovers – Sylvie Germain £8.99
Parisian Sketches – J.K. Huysmans £6.99
Là-Bas – J.K. Huysmans £7.99
En Route – J.K. Huysmans £7.99
The Cathedral – J.K. Huysmans £7.99
The Oblate of St Benedict – J.K. Huysmans £7.99
Lobster – Guillaume Lecasble £6.99
The Mystery of the Yellow Room – Gaston Leroux £7.99

The Perfume of the Lady in Black – Gaston Leroux £8.99
Monsieur de Phocas – Jean Lorrain £8.99
The Woman and the Puppet – Pierre Louÿs £6.99
Portrait of an Englishman in his Chateau – Pieyre de Mandiargues £7.99
Abbé Jules – Octave Mirbeau £8.99
Le Calvaire – Octave Mirbeau £7.99
The Diary of a Chambermaid – Octave Mirbeau £7.99
Sébastien Roch – Octave Mirbeau £9.99
Torture Garden – Octave Mirbeau £7.99
Smarra & Trilby – Charles Nodier £6.99
Manon Lescaut – Abbé Prévost £7.99
Tales from the Saragossa Manuscript – Jan Potocki £5.99
Monsieur Venus – Rachilde £6.99
The Marquise de Sade – Rachilde £8.99
Enigma – Rezvani £8.99
Micromegas – Voltaire £4.95

Anthologies featuring French Literature in translation:

The Dedalus Book of French Horror: the 19c – ed T. Hale £9.99

The Dedalus Book of Decadence – ed Brian Stableford £7.99

The Dedalus Book of Surrealism – ed Michael Richardson £9.99

Myth of the World: Surrealism 2 – ed Michael Richardson £9.99

The Dedalus Book of Medieval Literature – ed Brian Murdoch £9.99

The Dedalus Book of Sexual Ambiguity – ed Emma Wilson £8.99

The Decadent Cookbook – Medlar Lucan & Durian Gray £9.99

The Decadent Gardener – Medlar Lucan & Durian Gray £9.99

'Carmen!'

The shout cut through the crowd. It was icy cold and an ill-tempered wind was buffeting the people outside the *Sepu* department store, knocking them into each other in a tangle of inside-out umbrellas and flapping raincoats. Some, hesitating by the entrance, in the of warm air from the ventilating system, couldn't bring themselves to step out and face the rigours of the wintry street, while others, with feet like blocks of ice and clothes dripping, were vainly trying to push their way in.

Jostled from all sides, she tried to see where the shout had come from, to see if it was indeed directed at her. It was that particular hour of the day when the light is hazy and, despite the neon advertisements and the headlamps of the cars constantly sweeping past, the osmosis between departing day and falling night makes visibility poor, if not impossible, for the short-sighted. Carmen was short-sighted.

Her glasses were steamed up. Clumsily she wiped them. She felt slightly constricted in her tight coat and the detachable fur collar was irritating her. Making an ungainly movement, she dropped the parcel she was carrying. She scanned the noisy, heaving, sodden mass of people milling round her anxiously, but could not see anyone.

Ponderously, she bent down to pick up her parcel.

That was the moment when Dorita lost sight of her. With determined use of her elbows, she managed to force her way through the protesting crowd. She gave a little wave to show where she was. The glittering chink of her gold bracelets above the heads of the throng fascinated her, she never tired of it, but a stronger gust of wind almost blew off her headscarf.

That's the thousand pesetas for my shampoo and set down the drain, she thought.

Finally she saw her, crouching down, in a coat of indeterminate colour.

'Carmen! *Chica!*' Dorita cried, plunging through the crowd towards her.

She gave her arm an encouraging, familiar squeeze, forcing Carmen to stand up and making her drop her parcel again.

Her glasses were misted over with the rain, the same rain that emphasised the shadow of the moustache she had recently shaved. She heard the voice again, a slightly cracked voice, wavering between high and low, accompanied by a pain shooting up her arm, rousing long-buried memories.

'It's me, Dorita. Don't you remember me? Of course, it's been so long . . . People change, don't they?'

'Dorita . . . Good Lord, I didn't recognise you.'

Swiftly Dorita stooped down and picked up the parcel. Carmen lifted up her round face, its coarse complexion covered in a fine layer of sweat, and smiled gratefully.

'How on earth did you recognise me? What a memory, Dorita, what a memory, after all these years . . .'

The poor girl's even uglier than she was at school, Dorita thought to herself. Out loud she said, 'But darling, you've hardly changed. The moment I saw you I said to myself, that's my old friend Carmen, Carmen Gonzalo y Gonzalo.' She pursed her thin lips, with their overgenerous coating of Revlon lipstick, in the semblance of a smile.

'This isn't the market square, you know,' a man barked, pushing them unceremoniously aside.

'What a boor! Come on, Carmen, let's go and find somewhere nice and quiet for a chat. I presume you've nothing special on and, really, the man's right, this isn't the place to talk, what with the wind gusting like this. But still, what an ill-mannered . . .'

'Paloma's expecting me, the children . . .'

'The children? Paloma has children? She finally got married? It can't be true! Paloma married! I can hardly believe it!'

'Yes, she's married.'

'To that boy, what was he called now? You know, tall, strong – looked a bit like Rock Hudson?'

'No! Not like Rock Hudson!' Carmen exclaimed, suddenly firm. Then, unveiling the perfectly white and very extensive set of teeth that served as a smile, she added that he was a lot less good-looking and was called Paco, Paco Ramos.

'Oh yes. Funny, isn't it?' Dorita murmured, her tone suddenly a little distant.

'I can see you better now. Let me give you a kiss, Dorita.'

She rode the sticky impact without batting an eyelid. 'How about going to the *Galerias* for a little something?' she suggested, curious to know how Paloma, almost as ugly as her sister and lumbered with a silly mother, had managed to get married. It was a miracle, no more and no less.

'Great idea. After all, it's only a quarter to six and if I'm not there for the eight o'clock mass, Henriqueta can take the children with her. It's not often I go out, just this once won't do any harm.'

Dorita tottered along on her high heels, her stockings slipping down in damp wrinkles over her ankles. A fawn mink coat emphasised the plump curve of her buttocks, making her look even shorter than she was.

With her feet firmly ensconced in masculine lace-up shoes under transparent plastic overshoes, Carmen had a strangely slow, lumbering gait.

Dorita kept blinking. She was very short-sighted too, but vanity dictated that she never wore her glasses in public, only using them in the darkness of a cinema or for some particularly choice intellectual moment: glasses left on a book such as *The History of Philosophy in the Middle Ages* when visitors were expected, for example. More prosaically, though, they slipped off her short, flat nose each evening as she fell asleep reading an Agatha Christie while she waited for her husband. Carmen, of course, had no idea of that and, filled with wonder, clumsily stroked her friend's sodden mink as they walked along.

Straightening up, lifting her sagging bosom, Dorita asked, with a condescending smile, 'Beautiful, isn't it?'

'Oh yes. It must have cost a fortune.'

'It was for our twentieth wedding anniversary. That was five years ago –' She bit her tongue and quickly went on, 'This year I got a solitaire. Look.'

She struggled with her satin glove, finally managing to pull out a plump, slightly flabby hand on which liver spots were starting to appear. It flaunted a huge diamond.

'Look,' she repeated with a triumphant air. 'He asked me, "What do you want?" and I said, "It doesn't matter, as long as it's the biggest there is, at least the size of a chick pea."'

'Oh . . . so you got married to Polyto?'

Dorita did not hear the end of the sentence since she was brutally expelled from the lift of the *Galerias Preciados.* Ignoring the pushing, she put on a sparkling smile as she gave her friend her arm. Her complexion still had a semblance of youthfulness, thanks to the many skin creams, each more expensive, more revolutionary than the last, not to mention the hours spent in beauty salons. She shook her head and fluffed up her hair, which had been slightly flattened by the headscarf she had been forced to wear because of the weather. With a sigh of relief, she dropped onto the café chair, undoing her mink coat to reveal a silk blouse, slightly crumpled round the collar and stretched to the limit by the underwiring of a well-filled and expensive brassiere.

Her cheeks suddenly flushed bright red. Fanning herself with her hand amid the clatter of cups, the hubbub emanating from gaggles of middle-aged women round tables overflowing with good things, she said, 'I think I'd be better taking my coat off, the air-conditioning's terrible here. I've told the waiter often enough ...' – looking up – 'Yes, every Wednesday at seven I preside over a little gathering of friends, well, the wives of doctors, colleagues of my husband's, it's a chance to get away from everything, the children, the house, no need to spell it out, you'll know how it is yourself...'

'I almost never go out,' Carmen replied.

'Aren't you going to sit down?' Dorita asked, since Carmen was still standing at the table.

'Yes, yes, of course. I was just looking at you. I didn't recognise you.'

'I've changed, haven't I? The years don't pass without leaving their mark on us women ...'

'Oh no, it's not that. That's not what I meant, not at all,' Carmen hastened to add as she sat down, hampered by her parcel and the ultra-modern design of the chair, which refused to slide back on the thick carpeting, despite the thumps she gave it, and slightly embarrassed by the pool of water spreading round her shoes.

'Oh, but it is. Don't worry, I know how things are. I'm not the woman I was any more. Waiter!'

'I . . .'

'What do you want to drink? That's all right, think it over. As for me, let's see . . .' A broad smile revealed a set of teeth once perfect, now somewhat put in the shade by the shining gold of the extensive bridgework. 'A vodka orange. I usually stick to mineral water, because of the calories, or a nice hot coffee when it's really cold, apparently it burns off the fat, the Americans . . . well, you know, you read all sorts of things . . . But today we're celebrating, don't you agree? We must celebrate meeting again after all these years.'

'Of course, Dorita. You are in high spirits!'

'And why not?' she said, slightly embarrassed by her friend's tone of voice and the arrival of the waiter. 'The waiter's here. What do you want?'

'A chocolate.'

'Come now, Carmen, what about your figure? You ought to watch what you eat too. It looks to me as if you've got a bit of a spare tyre . . . Unless it's that coat.' She pursed her lips. 'Let me be frank with you – after all, that's what friends are for, aren't they? Well darling, I have to say . . . that coat doesn't suit you at all, not at all. You ought to try . . . I mean . . .' She was struggling for words. 'Perhaps you're right, after all. Deep down you've always been right, we should forget all this vanity about our appearance, it's the mind that counts, and as far as the mind is concerned, you've always had plenty, and some to spare.'

The waiter started to move away but her shrill voice brought him to a halt. 'Bring us some pancakes as well, and some whipped cream, yes, and a large pot of honey.'

He came back to the table, detached, silent, to note down the rest of the order. As he leant down he could not repress a smile contorted by weariness and Dorita gave Carmen a little sign. He scribbled something, slipped the note under the cloth and picked up the parcel.

'If you'll allow me . . .' He picked up her coat

with his fingertips and placed it elegantly on the empty chair.

Carmen blushed with embarrassment. Then, suddenly emboldened, she put her handbag and her string shopping bag, which had been slipping off her knees, on the chair too.

A strange silence fell on the café. The dozens of old, lipsticked mouths, which, until a moment ago, had been blowing out the bluish smoke that permeated the air, were now busy chewing on tarts and foie gras sandwiches, while their long American cigarettes smouldered in the ashtrays.

Dorita waved her hand to fan herself again. Her podgy arm was covered in gold bracelets. Carmen could not see them, having taken off her glasses once more, as they needed cleaning, but she could hear the faint jingling, which in her mind merged with the banal noise of cups and teaspoons.

Suddenly Dorita became aware of Carmen's mousy grey locks dangling down from her round head and looked about the room anxiously before giving a sigh of relief. Nobody. No one she knew in sight.

She felt slightly irritated with herself. And with her friend, who was now taking a man's handkerchief – a dirty handkerchief – out of her bag to wipe the lenses of her spectacles.

'Stop! You'll never get anywhere with that. It's disgusting.' And she pressed into her hand a little scrap of fragrantly perfumed, gauzy material, which Carmen had difficulty recognising as a handkerchief.

'Oh, thanks. How elegant, Dorita. But then, you always were, even at high school . . .'

'Shhh!'

The waiter was coming to the table.

'Thank, you. Just put it there, that's right, it's fine like that,' she said, to get him out of the way as quickly as possible.

Then, leaning towards her friend, 'What on earth made you go shouting things like that from the rooftops?'

'Things like what?'

'Of course, there was the civil war and we were patriots, but all the same! It's ancient history today and, as Juanjo says, what's the point of harping on about the same old stories, we must look to the future, the world belongs to the young . . . So anyway, I told them I was at the College of the Order of Our Lady of Mercy, until I went to university, you see it's . . . How shall I put it?'

'Them?'

'My friends, of course! The ones I meet here on Wednesdays. We have a little something to eat, just a hen party, and' – lowering her voice – 'the waiter might hear, you never know with these people from the lower classes. They still bear a grudge, what can one do, they have to be made to understand that they didn't win . . . So you can imagine they're not going to let an opportunity like that slip through their fingers.'

She leant back with a satisfied smile and went one, 'Yes, my friends, wives of colleagues of my husband for the most part,' – raising her voice – 'nice girls, the right kind, you know, I'm sure you'd like them.'

She bit her tongue. Why had she said that? What if Carmen were to take her at her word? Poor Carmen, so . . . so . . . How do you put it? An excellent woman, of course, but such a . . . And that's the way she'd always been.

Carmen, in some discomfort because the elastic of her suspenders was digging painfully into the soft flesh of her hips, was twisting and turning her heavy body in an attempt to free it. She started to sweat, then to smile, moving her neck from right to left for no apparent reason, as she had seen Dorita do. With what she intended as an elegant gesture, she waved her hand in front of her face, then grabbed the handkerchief, sniffing noisily. Dorita grimaced with disgust. Carmen, realising her faux pas, thought to remedy it by adding, in a loud voice, 'I'll wash and iron it before I let you have it back.'

'Yes, fine, but aren't you going to drink your chocolate? It'll be getting cold. It's a funny thing, but this cold weather seems to give me a thirst – cheers.'

She clamped her lips to the rim of the glass then, rolling her eyes, tilted her head back and downed her vodka orange in one gulp.

'Aah! That's better. I must have been in need of a pick-me-up. The strain, if you only knew, Carmen poor thing, I'm exhausted, literally exhausted today.'

Smiling, Carmen munched her way through a pancake filled with honey.

'Waiter!' Dorita called, 'Would you bring us a jug of water and two glasses? It's stifling in here . . .' adding, as he left, 'and a vodka orange.'

Then, turning to her friend, 'There's nothing better for quenching your thirst, you know, Juan Manuel, a friend, a very dear friend of my husband's, he's something high-up in export, travels a great deal, in fact his wife's always complaining, "He travels around so much, he's as good as never here," well, he always tells me, on the first of each month, oh, just a little dinner party we give for close friends, it's become a tradition almost, fourteen of us in all, more than that and the servants couldn't cope nowadays, "Dorita my lovely –"' she gave a skittish giggle, 'he always calls me that, "Dorita my lovely –" oh, men! You never know what's going on in their minds, if I'd wanted, Carmen, if I'd wanted . . . But, as the Virgin's my witness,' – she sketched a brief sign of the cross over her bosom and, to show her sincerity, placed her thumbs together and kissed them – 'I'm not one of those women who . . . you know what I mean.'

'Of course, Dorita.'

An irresistible surge of warmth swept through her. 'You know what? You must come to the house. Absolutely. I'll introduce you to my husband and the children.'

'I'd love that, of course. But I hardly ever go out, you know, the children . . .'

'Yes, yes, but we can make arrangements. Now where was I? Oh, yes! There's nothing better for quenching your thirst than a vodka orange, and what's more it burns off the fat.'

Carmen ran her myopic gaze over her friend. 'But you're not fat, Dorita, you know, at our age . . .'

'"At our age!" Oooh, listen to her! Aren't we getting philosophical. But we're not the same age, my dear, not at all. Tell me now, how old are you?'

Carmen thought she remembered she was younger than Dorita. She even had the feeling she'd left school before her. But it was so long ago, she might very well be mistaken.

'I'm coming up to fifty-six. Time simply flies.'

'You see? There you are!' Dorita exclaimed

triumphantly. 'Just what I was saying! Fifty-six! Let's see now, Paloma is two years younger than you, stop me if I'm wrong, and Henriqueta, Henriqueta – come on, let's have another drink to stimulate the memory – she must be the same age as ... no, poor Guille died when he was around forty and I was in Paloma's class and ...'

'That was when she came to live with Mama, a real saint. We were only little, Paloma and me, Papa had died six months before and Henriqueta –'

'Yes, yes, I know. But just let me think. She must be seventy-one at least.'

'She was seventy-two last September. She went on a trip. She'd earned it, she'd never been away on holiday and with my double salary for July and contributions from all the others, she went on a pilgrimage to Lourdes with Father Juan. If you'd seen how delighted she was! At first she didn't want to go, you know her, when summer comes she always says, "Go away? Me? What ever for? I'll close the balcony shutters, get out my little chair, my fan and the day's copy of *El Alcazar* and you can keep your holidays. That's my holidays, when the children are away" – I mean Paloma's children, of course, because I . . .'

Carmen blushed. But Dorita wasn't listening, immersed as she was in tortuous calculations: if she thought a bit, she would realise I'm approaching fifty-eight. My God! How awful! Doesn't time fly!

'. . . because I' – Carmen's voice faded to a faint tremor – 'you know, Dorita, I never got married. I just couldn't have.' She placed her hand on her breast in a melodramatic gesture that passed unobserved.

Dorita, more than happy to change the subject, assumed she had finished. A most disagreeable subject, if truth were known. Why on earth did she have to bring up that sordid question, she thought, frowning to show she was in a bad mood. After all, age doesn't really matter, it's the heart that counts, and at heart I'm a young girl. It is important for some people, of course – for her, for example, she really ought to have a look at herself in the mirror . . . at her age! It wasn't as if it was something new either, even at school she looked so much like an old maid people were already saying, 'her rice's been cooking too long.' She didn't fool anyone, certainly not me. Whereas in my case age, a *certain age*, simply indicates my social position: a husband, children, a chalet in the mountains, servants, my lifestyle, it's patently obvious, really.

She snuggled voluptuously into her fur to finish her drink, a satisfied smile on her face.

Carmen had closed her eyes, waiting for a response which never came, a comment, perhaps even a question. She had kept her hand on her breast, slightly tensed, in an attitude she imagined was both modest and rapt. As the silence continued, she opened her eyes. Dorita was slightly flushed, her eyes, once so bright, were underlined by voluminous purplish bags, her lips pale, the crimson Revlon now adorning the rims of the empty glasses cluttering up the table.

Feeling herself observed, Dorita gave a start. 'I was dreaming,' she said in a roguish voice, 'foolish things from a different age. But tell me, my dear, what about you? What have you been doing all this time. All right, let's make a pact: we won't talk about time any more. You've finished your chocolate? Waiter!'

'Yes, but –'

'No buts about it! To seal a pact you have to drink to it, don't you?'

'I don't know . . .'

'Oh come on now, don't be stupid! You have this terrible habit of pretending you're stupid when you and I both know you're not at all.' She smiled and gave her hand a squeeze. 'Waiter!'

Busy tidying up the crockery and cutlery, he looked round and came over with the easy movements of a dancer.

'Madam?' He leant forward gravely, as if to hear a confession, enveloping the table the two women were sitting at in a sudden halo of silence. Flattered by this mark of deference, Dorita smiled, a smile that was both condescending and imperious.

'Clear away these . . .' – she pretended to be searching for the word – 'these dead men. Dead men, Carmen. That's a good one!'

She burst into a deep, hoarse laugh. The waiter stood there, impassive. When her laughter subsided, she gestured vaguely in the direction of the empty glasses. Then she sighed, 'It's stupid, I know, but I can't resist a witticism, that's why Juanjo married me, for my mind . . . Though just between you and me, I don't believe it. If that were true, then the men would only marry those silly girls who fritter away their youth in the university lecture theatres, which clearly isn't the case, but you know . . .'

Carmen's face closed like the metal shutters they pull down over shop windows at the end of the day.

Realising her mistake, Dorita took her hand, murmuring in a tone of voice that was intended as sympathetic, 'Oh, I'm sorry darling, that's not what I meant to say . . .'

'No need to excuse yourself. It's what everyone thinks, I know.' There were tears in her eyes.

'No they don't. It's only fools who think like that.'

'But you just said it!' She felt an uncontrollable tickle in her nostril, a desire to blow her nose.

'But you misunderstood me, I assure you . . .'

'You said it.' She took out her handkerchief, her large man's handkerchief, with a stubborn expression on her face.

'All right, yes, true, I have to admit that in a certain sense I did say it.'

'There you are!'

Carmen was interrupted by a quiet clearing of the throat and she went bright red when she became aware of the presence of the waiter, who was still there, the tray balanced on the end of his arm.

Dorita quickly took the situation in hand, addressing him sharply. 'Well? What are you doing standing there like a lamppost?'

With a resigned air, the waiter shrugged his shoulders. He did not answer, but made as if to move off, presumably knowing full well he would not leave without a new order.

'Well, at least make yourself useful and bring us two martinis.'

'Very well, madam.'

'But I never drink alcohol.'

'Exactly. It's not alcohol. It's a pick-me-up.' In a louder voice: 'Very dry! – Anyway, if you don't drink it's a good opportunity to start. Now what I was going to say . . .'

A tear ran down Carmen's cheek, trembled on her lip and splashed down onto the tablecloth.

'Oh come on now, don't cry. I tell you there's no need to cry.'

'You said it!' She burst out sobbing.

Dorita looked round in alarm. Really, what a brilliant idea it had been to bring her here! Though actually it was a stroke of luck, she couldn't have foreseen this and if they'd been at the *California*, a smart place, always full of the young set and people of refinement, nostalgic for another age, another life, they would certainly have met Adela. Fat Adela who went there every single day to stuff herself with cakes.

A louder hiccup than the rest jolted her out of her reverie. She had to do something. Several amused and intensely irritating glances had already aroused her sense of decorum. The convulsive jerks caused by Carmen's sobbing were sending her greasy locks bouncing up and down; her chest heaved like a shapeless old bolster.

Overcoming a brief spasm of disgust at the

idea of touching her, Dorita took off Carmen's glasses, holding them in the tips of her fingers.

'What are you doing, Dorita, I can't see anything,' she stammered.

'That doesn't matter, you must calm down now, I'm going to . . .' She spoke in a firm, almost maternal tone.

'You said it,' Carmen repeated.

'Aaaahh! Enough is enough! You're starting to get on my nerves. All right, I said it! Yes, I said it and I'll say it again.' She had put the glasses down on the table and was looking at her with a hard, defiant stare, her podgy forearms resting on the tablecloth.

Dumbfounded, Carmen abruptly stopped crying.

'Ah, that's better, we're calming down, now we're showing a bit of decorum.' Then, as the waiter arrived, 'Thank you. You can put the glasses there.' Seeing him laboriously note down the order, she couldn't resist declaring, with malicious irony, 'You needn't worry, my friend, I'm not one of those women who leave without paying.' And to humiliate him even further, she added, in an aside to her friend, but loud enough for all the customers to hear, 'It appears any shortfall is deducted from their wages.' Turning to him, she went on, 'Off you go then, or isn't my word good enough?'

He said nothing and left, followed by dozens of glances that were half-pitying, half-contemptuous, that ideal formula for right-thinking charity.

'What impertinence! Still, as I was saying, that's what they're like, you can't change them. But to get back to us two – come on now, drink. Try it, you silly goose, it's not poison, just a delicious dry martini.'

With a grimace Carmen docilely moistened her lips.

'There! It's good, isn't it?'

'Yes, Dorita.'

Suddenly giving her hand a squeeze: 'That's what I like to hear.'

'Yes, Dorita.'

'So now let me explain –'

'No, please, I behaved like a little school-girl.'

'No, no, there must be no misunderstanding between us, I can explain –'

'I'm really sorry, Dorita, you're such a good friend.'

'And that's the very reason why –'

'No! I'd feel ashamed, I assure you. I don't know what came over me.'

'No, no, it's perfectly natural, I'm too brusque, I'm always very blunt. Juanjo often tells me, "You don't have to be so frank, Dorita, not so frank. You're worth your weight in gold, pure gold, and you don't cast pork before swine." But what can I do, I've always been like that. It must be my upbringing.'

And as if she suddenly found something extremely appealing in this idea, she emptied her glass in one gulp and added, delighted with herself, 'Yes it's a question of upbringing.'

'But I assure you –'

'Not another word or I'll get angry.'

'All right, if you insist, Dorita.'

'The thing is, I was only talking about those girls who go to university just to find a husband, who have no interest in what they're supposed to be studying and, what's more, don't actually manage to get their man either.'

'But –'

'Yes, I know what you're going to say. I only stayed there for six months, but what could I do? Juanjo was so urgent . . . it would have been a sin. It must have been love at first sight.'

She raised her eyes to heaven, then, lowering them again, her cheeks on fire, delivered the decisive thrust: 'Anyway, don't forget, you said yourself that you just couldn't have got married.'

Astonished, Carmen asked, 'But how do you know?'

'But, darling, you said it yourself only a few minutes ago, didn't you?'

'Yes, Dorita.'

'You see.'

'Yes, Dorita.'

'You just couldn't have got married.'

'No, I couldn't have got married.'

Carmen, her mind suddenly blank, stared at her glass, overcome with an inexplicable feeling of sadness. Her stare was so fixed it became painful and, shaking her head as if to rid herself of black thoughts, she forced herself to drink. She drank without enjoyment, looking in vain for the warming, fortifying effect of the fiery alcohol she had so often read about in books. But the taste in her mouth was the dry bitterness of a transient despair.

Sometimes, after a day which had been worse than others and her head felt as if it were about to explode under the pressure of the constant thankless struggle with pupils whom, deep down inside, she loathed, she would sit down at the table with the brazier underneath, put her swollen feet up on the red-hot grill and doze in the stuffy air of the room until dinner time.

Dorita slumped back and shivered in the icy silk of her blouse. She felt she must look drawn and was conscious of her foundation cracking into slightly dry patches, of the lack of lipstick revealing fine lines, of the irritation making her eyes water. Mechanically, she picked up her glass. The ice-cubes chinked in a spurious suggestion of gaiety.

She looked up and saw Carmen clasping her

empty glass in her hands. She had such a vacant, weary air that for a brief moment Dorita felt very close to her, almost ready to give her a hug, not for any special reason, the kind of hug that lets the other know you know, but it's not really important, just two girls together. The prelude to future sensuality. A mute plea before a maths test you haven't had time to revise because you spent half the night waxing your legs. But all that was far away, much too far away. Gone the days of the stinking spirit-stove and the impossible contortions required to reach the hair at the top of the thigh, just below the crease of your buttocks. Nowadays a young woman applied, silently and precisely, thin, disposable five-centimetre-wide strips of wax 'to discourage the growth of unwanted hair'. A low-temperature, plant-based wax. A unique wax.

She sighed. A different age.

Carmen gave an alarmed, slightly embarrassed smile.

'I'm sorry, Dorita, I . . . I don't know what came over me.'

'No need for excuses, we all have our moments of fatigue. It must be hard, mustn't it? And here am I stopping you going home for a rest.'

She had adopted an arch tone, emphasised by the pout of her delipsticked mouth.

'No, no! You mustn't think that,' Carmen protested vehemently.

'But of course I am. Don't worry, I can tell . . . Let's have another drink so you can forgive me.'

'No! No . . . You know . . .' She looked round with a worried glance and lowered her voice. '. . . it can't be cheap here. Why don't you come to our house? We can have a nice milky coffee.'

Dorita burst out into shrill laughter, full of justified satisfaction. 'Don't be silly. it's my treat.'

'Oh no. We must go halves.'

'That's enough, now let's drop this silly argument. Waiter! I've got plenty of money. You don't believe me?' – she started to rummage in her handbag – 'There, see . . . look. Look!'

She produced a red leather wallet, slightly worn but of excellent workmanship, so full of bank-notes it was impossible to close.

The waiter stood behind her in silence.

'I believe you, I believe you,' said Carmen, looking up at him, slightly embarrassed.

'Ah, back again, are you?' She gave him a cold stare. 'Bring us the same again . . . but two each. That way he won't come pestering us every five minutes.'

She burst out laughing. Her neck swelled and went bright red, while her body was racked with spasms. Carmen kept her eyes firmly fixed on the floor.

'You know, Dorita, we've already had a lot to drink. Perhaps –'

'A lot to drink?! A lot to drink?! Nonsense! You don't know what you're talking about. You have to get out, my girl, or in no time at all you'll find you're a slave. You have to learn to enjoy life while there's still time . . . Talking of which' – she made an effort to pull herself together – 'you work, don't you?'

Carmen broke into a delighted smile before replying, 'Yes! At a high school. I teach biology and –'

Dorita broke in. 'How very interesting.' She emphasised the word, drawing it out languidly so she could keep speaking. 'Actually I've always envied you, Carmen.'

'Me?'

'Yes. I often say to Juanjo –'

Carmen looked round at the decor of geometrical mirrors, set in walls covered in brown and orange fabric, reflecting the hazy silhouettes of dozens of women, inhaled the polluted, overheated air, took her courage in both hands and asked, 'But who is Juanjo?'

'What do you mean, who's Juanjo? My husband, of course. Who do you think he is, for goodness sake?'

'So you didn't marry that boy . . . Polyto?'

Dorita turned crimson, shook her head, sending her shampoo-and-set flying, and glared at Carmen, a look of contempt on her face. 'Of course I didn't! He's nothing but a paltry, third-rate lawyer.'

'So he did manage to qualify as a lawyer after all?'

Dorita's irritation was beginning to show. 'Obviously! But that's not the point. A girl owes it to herself to take a practical approach to life, especially a girl like me, not bad looking, from a certain social class ... and that, you know, is the crucial point,' – she paused for a few seconds – 'to maintain one's social status.'

'But I thought his family was ...'

'Yes, yes, of course. But for all that he was just a petty provincial lawyer.'

'I always thought he lived in Madrid ...' Seeing the furious look Dorita was giving her, she fell silent.

'I had to choose. Love, love, it's a fine thing but it's always the same: you go through the whole palaver, the big promises, the fine words, just to end up – pardon my French – with a prick between your legs.'

Carmen blushed scarlet. Dorita continued, raising her voice, filled with a mounting sense of certainty. She was in possession of the truth, a truth people did not always want to tell, and above all not to hear to go by the disapproving looks from the nearby tables.

'I don't know what there is to look so shocked about. You're not a fifteen-year-old girl any more and you teach biology into the bargain.'

She sipped her drink, which only served to spur her on. 'Now if this prick . . . All right, I'll put it in veiled terms, otherwise I have the feeling you're going to be sick. Everyone has to eat, don't they? Well I prefer to do it with a silver spoon rather than a wooden one. Really, I'm disappointed with you, Carmen, I didn't think you were so . . . Well, that's your affair.' She twisted her glass round in her hands. 'So I married Juanjo. A doctor. He's in a different league. Consultations, no more than fifteen minutes listening to the patients moaning and that's another tidy sum, on the nail, no questions asked. It's like magic! Not to mention the presents. Hams at Christmas – and the quality! Not what you get in the shops, I can assure you, direct from farm to table. And the casks of wine . . .' Emotion crept into her voice. 'He's a real democrat, is Juanjo, so close to the people, to the peasants, you just have to know how to talk to them. He loves them and they show their gratitude.' A sigh. 'Not to mention the hospital every morning and the Social Security in the afternoons, at siesta time!' She gave a laugh. 'I can tell you a good one about that, between ourselves, of course.'

Carmen leant forward to hear better.

'He never goes!'

'He never goes?'

'No!'

With a triumphant air, Dorita set about her second glass.

'But that's not possible, that's . . .'

'Really, you have to have everything spelled out.'

'I'm almost never ill, you know.'

'That's no reason. Do you think *they* are?'

'Who?'

'All those disgusting old men who go to the dispensary with their prescriptions, of course . . . Revolting! Yeuch! At the beginning, the first time, I went with Juanjo. He had to see for himself how things were done there. You can imagine what he was faced with. It was horrible. And then there are people who say doctors earn too much.

'When I tell you we had to send everything to the dry cleaners, absolutely everything. As far as our underwear was concerned, it was simple: straight into dustbin. As a precaution, you understand?'

She threw herself back in her chair, pale in her mink coat.

Carmen had leant forward, her chest resting on the table, lips parted, agog for what would come next.

'Disgusting. It still gives me the shivers just thinking about it. You're not drinking?'

'No, not just at the moment . . .'

'Well then I'll drink it. It'd be pity to let it spoil, it's like perfume, leave it exposed to the air for too long and . . . Disgusting! It shouldn't be allowed. An interminable line of old men, badly dressed, filthy . . . There's no law against being poor, of course, and we have to recognise that it's not entirely their fault. But still! There are limits!' She squirmed on her buttocks. 'Minimal standards, for heaven's sake. Now he pays a student to go down there. And he's doing him a big service. An act of charity. A third-year student, it's training for him, experience. The fifth years, on the other hand, had the effrontery to demand more or less the whole salary. Where will it all end? I ask you!'

Carmen did not reply. She would have very

much liked to ask her, but she didn't dare. How could she have, at least going so far as ... but that's the way things were. Life is full of mysteries, unfathomable mysteries.

'Not to mention the clinic ... he's a shrewd one, is Juanjo. But you're not listening?'

'Yes I am, I am listening.'

'So, you're teaching at a high school? Poor darling' – her tone suddenly softened – 'and here's me stopping you going home for a rest.' A tear ran down her cheek.

Carmen was shaken. 'Please don't cry, Dorita.'

'No, no, let me cry. Oh, I am selfish, so terribly selfish!' Sobbing, she collapsed onto the table, knocking over a glass.

Clumsily, Carmen tried to comfort her. Leaning on the counter on the other side of the room, the waiter was watching them. She thought she saw him smile.

The tables had gradually emptied, apart from one right next to theirs. At it an old woman was stuffing pieces of croissant dripping with milky coffee into her mouth and looking at them with a fierce stare.

'Please, Dorita, don't cry.' She looked round. 'Look, have a drink.'

She held out the last glass, her glass, still full of martini. Dorita drained it without stopping crying.

'You know I'm delighted to see you, to be out with you.'

'Is that true? You're just saying that because I'm crying.'

'Not at all! I don't get much fun out of life: school, the children . . .'

A glint of interest lit up in Dorita's eyes. 'You've got children?'

'Not me. Paloma. She's got seven. And they all come to the house. The poor woman hasn't got a life to call her own. So I take them after I've finished at school. It gives her a breather. Fortunately, thank God, I have a pretty robust constitution, even when I'm ill, when I have my –' She broke off, dumbfounded at what she was about to say in a public place, it must be the drink. 'You know what I mean . . .'

The martini had revived Dorita. With an amused look, she asked, 'What do I know?'

'It's not important. Anyway, no one believes me. They just can't believe I would need to take to my bed. Paloma would say, "What, take to your bed? You?" It happened once and she said, "You with your strong constitution? You're mollycoddling yourself, Carmen. We mustn't neglect the gifts God has given us." She called the children and they tickled and teased me to make me get up. All in good fun, of course.'

'I see. And did you get up?'

'It would have been unkind not too. Paloma, poor dear ... But still, I get such pains, every time.'

'Come now, Carmen, by your age you've stopped having periods.'

At the next table the old woman's mastication stopped and a silence like a scarlet casket enveloped Dorita's last word.

'Oh please, Dorita, not so loud. People will hear.' Full of shame, she lowered her eyes.

'Why should I not speak so loudly?' She raised her voice as she opened her bag to look for her compact. 'This is the twentieth century, Carmen. Why should we be ashamed? The times when women didn't dare speak of their periods are past.'

'For heaven's sake!'

'A load of nonsense! I'm not ashamed. I have my periods.' She looked at herself in the mirror and powdered her face copiously. 'At your age you shouldn't be living on illusions, Carmen, poor thing.'

The waiter was coming over, weary from a day that seemed to be going on for ever and sensing that the moment of departure had arrived.

'Yes, yes,' Carmen rejoindered hastily, 'I'm sure you're right.'

She fell silent, remembering the awful bleeding she was still subject to, all for nothing, and which caused her such terrible suffering.

Dorita closed her powder compact with a sharp snap. Now her lips were a deep, gaping wound in which the smile shone forth like a grimace suffused with cruelty.

'So we refuse to get old? You never cease to amaze me, never.'

The waiter was standing behind her. She was trembling with impatience and had to make an effort to control herself, to stop herself crying out loud.

The old woman passed their table, a gleam of contempt in her eyes.

Dorita rummaged round in her handbag with a pretence of absent-mindedness. Looking up, she smiled at Carmen. 'Go and powder your nose in the ladies', darling, it's fantastic what a difference a little powder can make to a woman.'

The waiter cleared his throat.

'What? Oh, it's you, you ... Off you go, darling. The gentleman is waiting.'

Carmen stood up obediently and set off for the ladies', her step slightly hesitant from tiredness and alcohol.

When she came back, feeling much better, she made a vague gesture in the direction of her coat. The waiter hurried over. 'If madam will allow me ...'

He picked up her coat and held it ready. Carmen, not knowing what attitude to adopt, just stared at it. Dorita burst out laughing. 'Get on with it. Put your coat on before the poor man gets curvature of the spine from holding it out like that.'

Head bowed, mortified and avoiding contact with the waiter's hands, she complied.

Dorita gave him a challenging look, waiting for him to help her on with her fur coat. Without lowering her gaze, she took several bank-notes out of her wallet and waved them at him. At that he came over, his face split by a smile as sharp as a knife.

She shivered at the touch of the man's icy skin on her neck. 'Come on, Carmen, it's getting late. Let's go.'

As her high heels sank into the thick carpet, she suddenly felt dizzy.

'What's wrong, Dorita?' Carmen grasped her arm with a look of concern.

One by one, with an inexorable crackling noise, the neon lights went out, plunging the large café, now empty, back into darkness.

'Nothing, nothing's wrong.' She jerked her arm away. 'What would be wrong with me? Come on, off we go. We've been hanging around here too long.'

Carmen followed, slightly behind, feeling humiliated.

Out in the street the flow of cars had lessened and the lights glistened joyously. The wind lashed the rare passers-by, making them walk at strange angles. The tailor's dummies in the window displays appeared to be watching them, ready to tag along behind.

She raised the collar of her fur coat with a very elegant, studied gesture. Not even looking at her watch, she exclaimed, 'Oh my God, it must be late! What will Juanjo say?' With a smile: 'He has his little habits, bad habits I've given him: he can't have his dinner without me.'

'The children! I must go and relieve Paloma, I really must! I'll take the Metro, I'll . . .'

'Don't worry, I'll take you home.'

'Oh no, I can't let you, your family'll be waiting, your husband. I don't want to make you late.'

'Well let them wait while I drive you home. You still live in the same place?' Not waiting for a reply: 'It'll only mean a slight detour, it'll be quicker, the car's parked just a couple of minutes from here.'

'You drive?'

'Who doesn't nowadays? Juanjo bought me a little car. Speed ... I love it.' She breathed in deeply. 'It's so intoxicating!'

'I'm sure you're right. Paloma's taken the test four times, but she's never passed.'

They were walking slowly, despite the cold, Dorita stopping at all the shop windows without looking at them, driven by an internal mechanism that defied logic.

'I'd have preferred white, but the salesman strongly advised against it, it gets so dirty in town,' she said, as they came to a red Seat. She opened the door and got in at the driver's seat.

Carmen went round the other side and waited, but her friend seemed to have forgotten her, immersed as she was in a final appraisal of her make-up, fascinated by her reflection in the rear-view mirror. Then she saw her open her handbag, take out her cigarettes, light one and abruptly sit back in her seat.

Carmen tapped on the window. Dorita put on a surprised look. 'Oh, I'm so sorry, darling, I'm so absent-minded ... and it's so cold! You could have caught your death. You should have given me a shout.'

'It doesn't matter.'

'Always holding yourself back, Carmen, putting other people first. You'll live to regret it one day, believe me, I know from experience.'

'No, no, I wasn't cold, I assure you, I was looking at the car, doesn't the paintwork shine . . .'

'You haven't shut the door properly. Do pay attention.'

She started the engine in a sudden fit of rage. They didn't say a word.

Broad avenues swept past. They ignored the trees making convulsive movements that were almost human along *Retiro* park.

Carmen relaxed, lulled by the sound of horns, the warm air from the heater and the softness of the seat, into which her weary body sank deliciously. Inside her head a vague feeling of remorse at not having gone home for the children, for the quarter-to-eight mass, gradually faded.

She was rudely awakened from her drowsiness by the brakes being slammed on. She looked at

Dorita, whose face, up against the steering wheel, was trembling; her voice was hoarse in a desperate effort to appear in high spirits.

'We're going somewhere! We can't part like this. It's unthinkable.'

'But . . .' Carmen wriggled in her seat, looking for words, worried.

'There's no but about it. If we don't take the opportunity now, when will we? Come on, be honest.'

'It's so late . . .'

'Late! Late! The night is still young. And me too. Look! Still lovely, aren't they?'

Without warning, she had opened her blouse, displaying the immense cups of her expensive brassiere in which two fleshy globes sat like two scoops of ice cream ready to melt down their cornet in the summer sun.

'Dorita! My God! Someone might see!'

Seized with an uncontrollable fit of giggles, Dorita, without looking behind, executed an abrupt U-turn, to a screech of tyres and blaring of horns.

She had not buttoned up her blouse and her

breasts were brushing against the steering wheel. From time to time a little giggle erupted from her clenched jaws, filling Carmen with apprehension.

'But where are we going?'

'A surprise.'

'I . . . I'm really not dressed for going out. I was just doing some shopping for Paloma and Henriqueta. Some limeflower tea from the herbalist's in calle de las tres Cruzes. Since we moved I'm the one who comes in to buy Henriqueta's herbal teas; coming into the centre's a real expedition for her now, poor woman, with her sight getting worse. She's a saint! You must come and see her, she often says, "What's become of Dorita? It's so long now since we saw her, she must have been gobbled up by wolves." She still remembers your mother – your poor mother, God rest her soul – coming to tell her, "Dorita simply must go to university but we can't really afford the text books . . . " And Henriqueta said, "That's no problem, Carmen will lend her hers." For her one book was the same as another . . . Of course, you didn't use them for long.'

'It was the philosophy course.'

'Yes, but you must come to the house, Henriqueta's bound to be in, she more or less never goes out, apart from mass every day.'

'I wanted to take law. The black gown's flattering.'

'Of course, but you got married too soon.'

'It was love at first sight.'

'Yes, love at first sight . . .' Carmen played with her string bag pensively. 'Just like me, exactly like me, only . . .'

'Where is this?' Dorita was driving almost at walking pace and screwing up her eyes to read the street names. 'Your sight's better than mine, what does that say, that sign?'

Carmen adjusted her glasses. 'Chemist's.'

'No. Next door.'

'Dino's Bar.'

The car swerved. 'No, that's not it. I must have got the wrong street. Still, my memory . . .'

'It was because of him I had to deny myself, give up lots of opportunities. Oh, don't I know it. After all, I was a young girl, just like all the rest, I had my chances.' Carmen gave a shrill laugh.

'What are you laughing at? You can't see

anything here. Look, there, the name of that street. What is it?'

'Calle Modesto Lafuente. After what I've been through, I couldn't marry another man, really I couldn't. It would have been like eating hard-boiled eggs without salt –'

'Ah, I think we're there.'

She braked to park the car. It was a dark street.

An illuminated sign lit up a small square of pavement where a man in livery was standing smoking.

'– insipid. I couldn't have got married after that. I simply couldn't have.'

'What that's you're muttering about? We're getting out. How do I look?'

She uncovered her teeth in a forced smile. Carmen started. 'Very nice. But where are we going?'

'Get out. It's a surprise.'

Obediently she got out. Dorita, who had set off towards the sign, turned round. 'Carmen, where are you going with that string bag?'

'I . . . I don't know. Should I leave it in the car?'

Dorita shrugged her shoulders and, with a look that brooked no resistance, tore the bag out of her hands, opened the car door and simply flung it onto the back seat.

'No more of this stupid nonsense now, eh? Follow me.' Then, softening, 'Give me your arm. It's better to go in together.'

Carmen looked round the empty street in alarm. Her body offered lethargic, passive resistance to the pressure on her arm with which her friend was pulling her, against her will, towards the square of light. She started a silent prayer. The door opened onto a deep, warm darkness. Carmen stopped.

'What is it now?' said Dorita in a low, fierce voice.

'Dorita . . .'

Her friend dug her fingernails into her hand. 'Come on. Stop behaving like a little schoolgirl, we're being watched. Move!'

Carmen closed her eyes. Terror flooded through her: ideas of the devil, of sin, sermons on repentance, conversations suddenly interrupted by her appearance, certain images in films that had escaped the censor's scissors, the disturbing sight of men's trousers in the Metro she could not take her eyes off, sudden hot flushes in her narrow bed on nights when she could not get to sleep. She stood there, unmoving, eyes closed, gripping her handbag, while Dorita took off her coat with the ease of an habituée and handed it to the cloakroom attendant, one eye already on the room hidden from view beyond a red velvet curtain. Soft music was coming from it. She pulled her skirt down, smoothed her blouse and threw out her bosom.

'Your coat . . .' The dreary, apathetic voice struck Carmen like an electric shock. Without really being aware of what she was doing, she put her hand to her collar to undo it. Dorita stepped forward, placing herself between the attendant's outstretched arm and her friend, and said curtly, 'The lady is keeping her coat.'

She thought of Carmen's dress, though, to tell the truth she could remember nothing precise about it apart from the smell of sweat held in by cheap deodorant.

'She's cold ... she doesn't feel too well this evening, do you darling? But she was so determined to come.'

Too drained by emotion, Carmen said nothing.

Dorita chose a table close to the bar with a sofa at right angles. She pushed Carmen in that direction and her friend collapsed onto it, her eyes fixed on her feet, only too glad to be in the shadow of the red spotlights, which lit up the room intermittently. The music came from loudspeakers cunningly concealed behind risqué engravings.

At the bar the bartender was going about his business sluggishly. The silence was interrupted by occasional chuckles or bursts of laughter coming from behind the screens.

After having scrutinised the surroundings, Dorita flopped against the backrest. 'Of course, I should have known, it's still too early. We've come much too early.'

'What?'

'Nothing. How could you understand? Forget it, let's order something to drink. Waiter!'

'Nothing for me, Dorita, please . . . I've drunk too much already . . . You know I –'

She swung round to face her. In a furious voice she murmured, 'Now you just listen to me. This isn't a cafeteria, even less a youth fellowship party, here everyone has to have a drink. Understand? You can't not order something.'

'Don't get angry. I didn't mean to annoy you, Dorita. Anyway, now I think about it, I am thirsty, I will have something, it's so hot . . . I know, a cola.'

'A cola!' she mocked. 'Why not a glass of ice-cold milk with a straw?'

Carmen made an effort and produced a smile. 'What marvellous ideas you have! And so original! A glass of ice-cold milk, that's exactly what I fancy, it's so hot in here . . . I'll take off my coat.'

'No! Don't even think of it,' Dorita commanded between her teeth, seeing the waiter approach. 'There's nowhere to put it and, anyway, you should never take clothes off when you're too hot. You might catch a chill or something.'

'What can I get you young ladies?' He smiled as he bowed.

Dorita sat up. 'I'd like one of your cocktails . . you know, the one with all the colours and an . . .'

'Olive! A San Francisco for the young lady.'

'Thank you.'

'And for madam?' With his chin he indicated the shadow huddled at the end of the seat. All that could be seen were two puffy red hands sitting on the table like two hunks of meat.

'The same,' Dorita hurriedly added.

Time passed. She was beginning to get a little edgy. Nothing, absolutely nothing worth bothering with, while only last week . . . but then she'd been with Paquita. She was quite a different kettle of fish to this . . . this . . . well, what was done was done. No comparison at all. Paquita had style, that was for sure. A bit vulgar maybe, her background, that kind of thing always comes out, but there was no denying she lured them. And then she, Dorita, with her air of natural refinement, her subtle, witty manner, she gave the evening a certain *cachet*.

Today though . . . Immersed in her thoughts, she almost failed to hear the sound of the door opening. Instinctively she stretched out her legs, still her trump card according to Juanjo.

They made a noisy entry, with roars of laughter. They seemed to be on the prowl, they noticed Dorita's legs immediately, a gleam of white in the pink half-light.

'I see the fair sex is here already,' said the younger of the two in a voice loud enough to be heard.

'Two Bamboos,' the other ordered.

They turned their backs to them for a while.

'Lend me your glasses,' Dorita whispered.

Paralysed by fear, boredom and fatigue, Carmen, who was stifling in her coat, did not hear and gave a cry of fright when she felt a hand snatch off her spectacles, abruptly plunging her into a misty haze fraught with danger.

Dorita swiftly put them on and turned to look at the two men leaning on the bar. With an expert eye she registered the impeccable cut of their suits, the expensive, if slightly worn shoes, the broad shoulders, the beginnings of a spare tyre. The younger seemed the more attractive, but from behind it was impossible to come to a definite judgment.

She turned to Carmen, voluble all of a sudden and full of restrained irritation.

'I don't know how you can put up with these glasses, darling, they're so heavy. Of course, not everyone's lucky enough to be able to see in the dark like a cat. You really ought to try some contact lenses, you must let me give you an address.'

Surprised, Carmen didn't know what to say, and reached out blindly towards her friend to get her property back.

The two men swivelled round on their stools. Dorita gave a shrill laugh and went on, in a girlish tones, 'You're priceless, Carmen, you really are. A real scream.'

The younger of the two men took out a packet of cigarettes and patted his pockets.

'Got a light?' he asked, giving his companion a wink.

'No. I think I must have left my lighter on the table in the restaurant. But why don't you ask these charming young ladies,' he added in a louder voice, 'I'm sure they will be kind enough...'

Carmen put her spectacles back on and leant forward towards her friend, intrigued by what she had just said. She found herself brutally pushed back into the depths of the sofa by hands whose sharp nails dug pitilessly into her bloated stomach. Seeing the man approaching, she stifled her protest.

'Excuse my presumption, señorita...'

'Señora, if you please.'

'Señora!? But that's impossible. You? To look at you I can hardly believe...'

'But I am.' She held out a hand on which the plain band of gold was almost completely hidden by the jewelled rings adorning her fingers.

He sketched a bow.

'I must bow to the truth, but such youth, such beauty... I can hardly restrain my admiration...'

'Please, señor!'

'Do forgive me. I don't want to pester you any longer, señorita... I mean señora. I just came to ask if you had a light, for me and my friend.'

Dorita raised a questioning eyebrow and assumed a surprised look. 'Your friend?'

'My God! Where are my manners this evening? I haven't even introduced myself . . . The odd glass too much, I'm sure you understand . . .'

She waved her hand in a gesture designed to suggest he was forgiven for what he had just said, that it was of no importance.

'Jorge, come over here a moment . . . Allow me to introduce ourselves, this is Jorge, my friend, we've known each other for ever –' he gave a laugh, '– and I'm Paco, Paquirri to my friends – Paquirri, like the toreador,' he added for good measure.

Jorge was in his forties, his jacket wide open to reveal a pale pink shirt bulging at the seams. He bowed.

Carmen started to tremble.

'Move along a bit, darling. Make room for these gentlemen.'

Dorita slid along the bench, doing so as agilely as she could. Jorge sat down opposite her. They struck up a conversation, a superficial exchange of courtesies and gallant compliments. The room was gradually filling up, couples disappearing behind the screens, single men nursing a drink at the bar, more rarely women – of the type who inevitably attract glances.

'But we haven't got anything to drink!' Dorita exclaimed. 'Carmen ...' she paused and sighed. 'Just before you arrived Carmen was saying she was dying of thirst.'

When three pairs of eyes peered through the gloom towards her, Carmen, her mind fuddled with drink, managed to control herself sufficiently not to cry tears of shame.

'After that I couldn't have got married,' she babbled tipsily, 'I simply couldn't.'

The burst of laughter that greeted this brought her fully awake and left her feeling even more humiliated.

'I'm going to get some cigarettes,' said Jorge, 'you give Dick our order, Paquirri.'

'Dick?'

'The waiter. We're regulars, so to speak, aren't we?' Paquirri replied with a grin. 'I'll order something very special, you'll be amazed.'

'We've already had too much to drink,' Dorita protested. 'You know ... to be perfectly honest

I have to admit I don't usually drink that much. This evening I've let myself be led astray ... Carmen ...'

Carmen, indignant, opened her mouth. Dorita quickly leant over to her and, as soon as the two men were far enough away, whispered in her ear, in a tone of feigned contrition, 'I know, I know what you're going to say, but you've got the wrong end of the stick, I assure you. They're nice, don't you think?'

'Who's nice'

'They are, who else! Sit up straight, they're watching. What style! You can see right away the kind of person you're dealing with. Real men, businessmen, who've been around, travelled a lot, used to dealing with important ...' – she looked for an adequate word – 'important deals. You know, company directors, entrepreneurs. Believe me, I've got an eye for that kind of thing. They're not a couple of skirt-chasers, out after one thing only. You know those awful types: "Hello. Yes or no?" Phew, it's stifling in here ...' She unbuttoned her blouse revealing a hint of cleavage. 'Ah, that's better. Now what was I saying?'

'That they're not a couple of skirt-chasers,' Carmen repeated dully.

'Skirt-chasers!? The things you say, Carmen!' She smiled into the surrounding darkness. 'But tell me about yourself. You were saying?'

'Aha, you girls having a heart-to-heart? I wouldn't want to interrupt,' said Paquirri, sitting down, the glasses in his hands.

'But you're not interrupting, not at all.'

'Oh, good. I'd find it difficult to abandon such charming company,' he said with a smile. He stretched his legs out under the table, accidentally brushing against Dorita's. She gave a start and opened her knees slightly.

'Oh, I'm sorry. It's so cramped.'

'That's all right. I was just saying the very same to my friend . . .'

She felt the man's knee slip between hers. Excited, but slightly shocked all the same, she decided not to let it show and said, pretending to scrutinise the drink he was holding out to her, 'It looks as if it's rather strong for a woman, don't you think?'

'Not at all. It sets you up. Drink it down and you'll see.'

She pursed her lips and placed them against the rim of the glass.

'No, not like that . . . down in one.'

He grasped the glass and leant forward, as if to help her to hold it, at the same time overcoming the weak resistance of Dorita's legs.

A little of the drink spilled over her breasts, wetting the material of her blouse. Without relaxing the pressure of his knee, Paquirri handed her a perfumed handkerchief, apologising profusely. All at once she blushed bright red.

'Yes, yes, it's all right . . . there's no need . . . it doesn't matter, come on Carmen, you have a drink too.'

'I . . .'

'As you like. If you're not going to drink it I'll have yours as well. Perhaps I should order something less strong for you?'

Summoning up all that was left of her courage, Carmen whispered, 'A glass of water.'

Dorita smiled. 'She's just a child.'

Paquirri looked at her with a free-and-easy stare.

'And she never could have got married, could you, darling?'

'No.'

'It was love, the real thing,' Dorita said with a mocking smile.

'Ah, the real thing! Only happens once in a lifetime,' he added in theatrical tones.

'He must have been very handsome, mustn't he?'

'Very handsome . . .'

'And tall . . .' Under the table Dorita opened her legs.

'Yes,' sighed Carmen, almost in a trance.

'It's important for a woman, a man's height,' said Paquirri sententiously.

'And you'd known him for a long time?'

'A long time . . . such a long time.' Carmen stared vacantly at the bar. 'I always knew him, I still do today.'

'But then why . . . ? No! What are you trying to tell me, Carmen? He didn't . . . ? My God, don't tell me he got married?'

Her eyes veiled with tears, Carmen nodded. 'In a way, he . . . he's not free. Not free for me.'

The man slipped his hand underneath the table and touched Dorita's knee.

'A married man!' she exclaimed, straightening up for a moment, only to return docilely to the contact of the man's hand.

'I loved him. Loved him very much.'

Encumbered by the table, he could get no further.

Dorita smiled, pretending to smooth down an errant lock of hair.

'I must look awful!' She stood up in a coquettish posture. 'I'm going to powder my nose.'

He watched her go. Jorge wasn't going to come back. He'd seen what was on offer and gone to try his luck elsewhere. The die was cast.

'He was so strong, so handsome, I loved him. I always thought that one day I would be the woman he would hold in his arms, the woman whose head would rest on his heart at dead of night, the woman whose face would lighten his darkness. How could I have married another?' She raised her voice. 'I ask you, Señor, I ask you. I am one of those women who are faithful. Faithfulness made woman! Despite all the years, all the years that have passed in vain, for me, for him, for both of us, I have always known, in my heart of hearts, in this poor heart of a loving woman, that he too was waiting, waiting for the other half of the orange.'

Dorita's silhouette had vanished between the draperies.

He continued to follow her progress beyond the burgundy velvet, which swayed slowly in the wake of her hips.

What was this bag lady drivelling on about? Paquirri instinctively shrank back slightly.

'He's with me all the time,' Carmen went on feverishly. 'He never leaves me. Here! Look!'

As he looked on in disgust, she started to root round in her bag with spasmodic movements, taking out an old wallet, from which she extricated a newspaper cutting yellow with age, grubby from contact with her fingers, sodden from the saliva on her lips. She pressed it to her heart, closing her eyes tight, with an intensity that was almost painful. Then, slowly, like the bride making her way up the aisle, she placed the photo on the table, a photo of Rock Hudson, taken from the film *A Farewell to Arms*.

Dorita had left the door ajar. Placing her handbag on the lavatory, she leant forward to adjust the attachment of her stocking to her suspender.

She did not hear Paquirri arrive. She saw his reflection appear in the mirror. Her fingers detached her stocking, which floated down to settle round her ankle.

'Oh!' She gave a little cry and quickly straightened up as she saw him come into the cubicle with an air of determination. She took a step back and smiled. The man sketched a vague gesture and leant against the door, which he had taken care to close.

'But what are you doing here? You must leave . . .'

'No need to be afraid, I won't do anything, I won't touch you, I'll just watch.'

Dorita put on a show of annoyance. 'Right then, it doesn't look as if I'm going to persuade you . . . But you have to admit it's hardly decent. You must promise not to look.'

The man appeared to laugh, but no sound came from his lips.

'At least, not to look too closely, I have to put my stocking back on and . . .'

'Put it back on, then, and stop making such a fuss,' he said curtly.

Somewhat taken aback, Dorita pretended not to have heard and bent down. She lifted up her skirt, revealing an expanse of fat, white thigh. The man did not move. She sighed.

'My God, isn't it hot in here?! It's so cramped . . . I'll never manage. You're in my way, standing there, saying nothing.'

The man did not reply. Thinking he suddenly felt shy, she lifted up her skirt a little farther.

'Juanjo tells me I have magnificent legs. He's crazy! Love makes you blind, but sometimes I tell myself he's not all that wrong. Have a look yourself. What do you think? Be honest now . . .'

The man was very pale. She went up to him.

'Of course there's so little light, you can't tell, you can't see anything. If you promise . . .'

'I'm not promising anything at all.' His voice was harsh, brutal.

'You frighten me, I . . . after all, we have to be able to trust each other. I know you, you're not like the others.' She took his hand. 'What cold hands you have. My skin's soft, isn't it?'

The man's stillness both irritated and excited her at the same time. Slightly embarrassed, she felt the coldness of his palm. She moved the inert hand towards the top of her thigh

'Cold hands, hot blood . . .' She giggled nervously. 'What was it I was saying . . . I still haven't got over the shock, have I? Oh course, beside a young girl of twenty . . . But you're not saying anything . . .' He had lowered his head and with her other hand she tousled his hair. 'You have a tender heart, I saw that straight away, you can't hide that from a woman. Oh, please don't, it's not right.'

She suddenly tore herself away from him, as if he had made a movement, and backed away towards the lavatory.

'Don't you realise, someone might come, anyone.' She took a step towards him again. 'But perhaps you find me intimidating, look me in the eyes . . .' She took his face in her hands, trembling slightly, her stocking still round her ankle. 'No, don't look at me like that. My God, what a terrible way of looking at a woman! It must be me . . . You're closing your eyes, how sensitive, it must be . . . No! We mustn't say anything that can't be taken back, something you might regret, something we might both regret, it's madness . . . So it's up to me to take the first step? Well then . . .'

Paquirri stood there under the neon light, unmoving, in the narrow space between the door and the lavatory, as Dorita, suddenly gripped by a feverish excitement, took off her blouse and let her skirt slip to the floor.

'Close your eyes. You're only to open them when I tell you, it's going to be a surprise.'

Meekly he obeyed. Dorita shivered, no longer feeling her clothes on her skin. She surveyed the towel hanging over the gilded rail, gauging its size.

Yes, it was definitely big enough to cover up that horrible neon tube. Then she would be able to loosen her brassiere, just a little. She was trembling violently. But she'd have to pull the little stool out from behind the lavatory to be able to reach it.

She turned round and looked at him. Pale, covered in sweat, his arms dangling down beside his body, he still had his eyes closed.

The perfect gentleman, she'd guessed that right away. Holding the towel, she started to climb up onto the stool, which seemed to be rather precariously balanced.

That was the moment when the man opened his eyes. Standing a little above him, she was teetering on the stool. Her buttocks, thanks to her panty girdle, which compressed her flesh, creating two rose-pink protuberances at the top of her thighs, formed an almost perfect circle. Her waist consisted of a succession of fatty folds, which reached as far as the solid barrier made by the elastic of her brassiere. He raised his arm, his hand brushed against one of the rolls of flesh. He shivered in disgust.

'Please, I beg you, you mustn't . . .'

His hand slipped gently down onto her girdle and he came up close to her. He touched the seams, feeling the threads. She gave a nervous laugh. 'You're tickling me.'

Having completed their exploration, the man's fingers came to a halt on the suspender, which was dangling limply on her thigh.

Dorita was vainly trying to fix the towel over the neon tube. If only she had some drawing pins, but obviously you can't think of everything, things weren't what they used to be, in the old days they'd really had time, time to live, but nowadays everything was getting terribly complicated, she should have thought of it . . . a single drawing pin would have done, even a safety pin or . . .'

The feel of the elastic was pleasurable and he started to pull on it, gently at first, then harder and faster, a smile slowly spreading across his pallid features. Taking a deep breath, he pulled it as far as it would go, down to the level of Dorita's knee. She lost her balance, crying out as she tottered.

Brusquely, the man pushed her with one hand, setting her back on her feet. His other hand released the suspender, which slapped painfully against her flesh with a brutal whiplash.

She gave another cry and fell onto him. The man reached up and grabbed the folds of flesh round her waist in his hands, pulling harshly at the skin.

'Ouch! You're hurting! Will you let go of me! Let me get down. I'm going to kill myself on this stool.'

'Stay where you are,' he said in a low, menacing voice.

Dorita did not know what to say. She stood there, motionless, keeping her balance. The mirror reflected her vast bosom, heaving as she breathed convulsively.

'Take off your brassiere.'

'No! ... You must ask me nicely. Otherwise ...'

He pinched her. She cried out.

'Give it me. Quick'

Somewhat anxious, she unhooked it and gave it to him, closing her eyes.

Her breasts tumbled down, landing with a soft slap against her stomach. He gave a short, sinister laugh.

Dorita did not know what to do. She waited,

passing her tongue backwards and forwards over her dry lips.

'You're terrible. A terrible man ... It's the first time. To think that I've had to wait so long before meeting you, so long ... But no one'll know anything, we'll keep our secret. We'll see each other and ...'

She tittered as she felt the man's hair brush the tips of her breasts, the man who had just knelt down.

'You're crazy, darling, here ... Just wait a moment, I'll take it off, it'll make it easier.'

The man started to smile. Dorita got down off the stool. She struggled with her girdle for a while, the sweat wasn't making things any easier, it just made the elasticated material stick even more closely to her skin. Eventually she managed it.

Hardly had she stepped out of the garment than the man threw himself at her. His eyes were shining and the strangely pointed tip of a pink tongue appeared between his teeth.

Dorita stepped back, simpering, 'Gently, darling, gently ... Theeere. We've all the time we need ... Whatever are you doing now? You're crazy. I ...'

The man was giving Dorita's hand, which she had modestly placed over the elastic of her panties, a vigorous licking. Slightly disconcerted, she tried to push him away. He started to grunt.

'Oh come on now, be sensible, I ... Stop it, please, my love, control yourself, can't you?' she begged, trying to hold him off. The man drew his face back a little from Dorita's stomach, muttered something incomprehensible then, with a brutal swoop, sank his teeth into her hand. She let out a muffled cry.

She shook her hand, trying to free herself, but the harder she shook it, the more he tightened the grip of his jaws. Her breasts were dripping with sweat.

The man grunted, biting and shaking his prey from side to side. Then he tired and stopped for a moment. He looked up. He was smiling.

Her eyes clouded with tears, Dorita made a valiant attempt to return his smile, aware that she was experiencing something exceptional. She sketched a caress. The man threw himself on her again. With a faint cry, she swiftly withdrew her bleeding hand. She was wedged in against the lavatory. The cold porcelain gave her a start.

'For the love of God, let me get out of here. What are you doing? Oh God, what are you doing?'

As she was trying to move, the man caught hold of one of her breasts and twisted it, thus immobilising her while he started to tear off her panties with his teeth.

A strong pair of panties, well made, of a material that was both hard-wearing and delicate, able to stand numerous machine-washes without losing their shape, a pair of panties that only yielded to the assaults of the man's teeth with the greatest reluctance.

Horrified, Dorita did not have the strength to cry out.

In a wild frenzy, he tore violently at the fabric until it finally gave way. He let go of Dorita's breast, which had gone a purplish shade, and, falling to the ground amid hoarse grunts mixed with laughs, started to gobble up the shreds of material greedily, whilst his legs jerked in frenetic quiverings.

Close to hysterics, she got into her skirt and blouse and, without bothering to put on her shoes, dashed out, stepping over the man, who by now was oblivious to her. Having consumed her panties, he was turning his attention to her girdle, seized with a fit of crazy, uncontrollable laughter.

Looking round one last time, she almost screamed. She swept past the waiter, throwing him a few bank-notes, which he picked up, an amused glint in his eyes.

Carmen, tired of waiting, had eventually fallen asleep, the photo in front of her on the table. She was brutally roused from her slumbers by Dorita shaking her and hurrying her up, not allowing her time to think, nor even to wake up properly.

'My photo!'

'We're leaving.'

'My photo! I want my photo.'

'That's enough,' Dorita yelled, already at the door. 'Let's get out of here.'

She dived into the car and started the engine, screaming, 'Get in, you idiot!'

Carmen hardly had time to close the door before she set off. The squeal of the tyres pierced her eardrums and set off floods of tears.

Dorita drove very fast, ignoring traffic lights and give-way signs, hunched over the wheel, dishevelled and breathing hard, her teeth clenched.

Carmen did not dare utter a word, closing her eyes in terror each time a horn broke the silence of the night with a honk of protest. In the middle of a brightly lit avenue Dorita suddenly slammed on the brakes and switched off the headlights. Carmen turned to look at her.

Her friend's face was in a frightening state: covered in long streaks of black and smudges of face powder, with lipstick smeared over her chin. She started to look for something in her handbag but then, not finding it, burst into tears.

'I've lost my handkerchief! Oh my God, where is it? Juanjo will never forgive me. Never! It was such a beautiful one, such fine material. Juanjo's very strict about things like that. No one knows that better than I do, no one believes me. Please God, let me find it again. Where can it be? Oh my God, he's going to be furious.'

'No one loses their temper over a handkerchief, Dorita,' said Carmen in schoolma'amish tones.

She turned on her in fury. 'And what do you know about it, eh? What could you possible know about beautiful things? You with your – '

'Oh please,' Carmen broke in apprehensively, 'don't get angry, I didn't mean to – "

'You didn't mean to, you didn't mean to . . . "I didn't mean to"! Pillar of the church! Sanctimonious prig!'

She burst out laughing, her face contorted with hate.

'You're just an old maid. That's it, a stupid old maid, bitter and jealous, jealous of me. That's what you are. And it's all your fault. I'll tell Juanjo. You'll see, you'll see! I don't want to see you any more. Get out. Get out of my car.'

Carmen stammered, 'But Dorita . . .'

'Get out of the car! I don't want to see you any more. It's all your fault this happened. A tart who hasn't the courage to do things openly, that's what you are. A pervert. But I saw that right away, oh yes . . . I'm going to tell Juanjo. I'm not going to stand for it! A tart, a pervert! Get out of my car! I don't want . . .'

Dorita started to scream, her face twitching with nervous spasms, her complaint degenerating into a string of insults.

Carmen, paralysed by the words she had heard, offered dull, passive resistance, but eventually she was forced to yield and get out of the car, which roared off, taking with it her string bag full of groceries and Henriqueta's herbal teas.

She thought she heard a demoniac laugh.

She stood there out in the road for some moments, petrified with fear at the pale shadows of the houses on the tarmac, at the distant twinkling of the stars, always assuming it wasn't the after-image of all the traffic lights they had gone through, flashing orange at this hour, putting the city at the mercy of any late-night maniac at the wheel.

Her mind a blank, she decided to cross the road, her instinct for self-preservation, as well as her fear and confusion, quickening her pace. She came to a bus stop. In relief she collapsed onto the little plastic bench and waited.

No one.

She stood up several times, scanning the darkness in the hope of seeing the reassuring massive silhouette of the vehicle. The neon light was making her eyes hurt and she was cold. A sharp, icy wind had got up. She looked at her watch: twenty to four. There wouldn't be any busses running. She certainly wasn't going to wait over two hours for the next one.

In desperation she started to walk, making a conscious effort to remember the route and going over in her mind the advice of her cousin, a policeman, on how to avoid being attacked: walk quickly, as if you know where you're going, neither too near to the buildings – you never know what the threatening shadow of the porches might conceal – nor too near to the road, where it is impossible to avoid the classic motorised purse-snatch.

Time passed. By the time Carmen saw her street day was breaking behind the trees motionless in their slow death, asphyxiated by carbon dioxide. A huge wave of relief sent the tears coursing down her cheeks and, her feet swollen by her long walk, she stumbled as she crossed the entrance.

What were they going to say? Henriqueta must be terribly worried. They would certainly have told Father Juan, the police ... A warm feeling flooded though her at a vision of the family gathered together, the image of dignified sorrow: the children asleep on the sofas, Paloma's husband, the sole male element apart from Father Juan, striding up and down, a grave look on his face, Henriqueta kneeling in prayer with the priest before the statue of St Anthony, Paloma curled up in an armchair, clutching a handkerchief sodden with tears.

Here I am, she would say, a miserable sinner.

And she would throw herself at their feet, begging their forgiveness. Henceforward nothing would be as it was before.

Nervously she slipped the key into the lock, it was time to bring their suffering to an end. She put on a pale smile.

Having made it to the car park of her apartment block without accident, Dorita took one last look at herself in the rear-view mirror. With a nod, she deliberately tore her blouse, then, placing her fingernails on her neck, scratched herself. Her face contorted in a brief spasm of pain, her eyes misted over. She would certainly manage a proper cry in his arms, but she could make doubly sure with one final scrape of her claws when the lift reached their floor.

She would leave her finger pressing on the bell-push till the door opened. Swaying, she would lean against him, murmuring, 'Juanjo, oh Juanjo,' and her only reply to his urgent questions, to the ashtrays overflowing with half-smoked cigarettes – unmistakable signs of the anxiety caused by the long wait he had had to endure – would be silence, interspersed with repeated moans, sobs, and his name recited like a Lenten rosary.

Later on, ensconced among some cushions, close to fainting, an eau-de-Cologne compress on her forehead, she would tell him everything and he would bury his unshaven face in her bosom.

Her tale of woe would move him to tears, he would call for vengeance. She would stroke his hair to calm him, she would tell him about the man and his obscene desires, about Carmen, that old bawd, that pervert soured by long celibacy, and the way she had abused her trust, her generosity. Hadn't she given her a sweet little chiffon handkerchief? Hadn't she invited her to the café at the *Galerias Preciados*? And how had she thanked her? She had dragged her off to that den of vice, had forced her to drink, drugged her probably, then delivered her up to the desires of a man, perhaps two . . . oh, Juanjo!

Then she would burst into tears.

The corridor was gloomy, Carmen could just make out the chairs along the wall.

They must be in the living room, but the light seemed to be out. She was struck by a thought that moved her: in the dark! They were waiting for her in the dark! Just as the early Christians had waited for their encounter with the lions, in the dark of their prisons, praying.

She approached quietly, placing her cheek

against the closed door to listen, to hear the the murmuring of prayers.

The lift doors opened and Dorita felt for the light switch with one hand. There was no point in hurrying. She tottered to the door of their flat, then quickly retraced her steps and set off again, in more dramatic mode this time. Juanjo must be at the door. From inside the flat the sound of the lift could be clearly heard. She felt she could see the door move; she put her hand to her brow and threw back her fur with a weary gesture.

Carmen opened the door and, closing her eyes, took one step forward before falling to her knees. Nothing happened, no one. Somewhat disappointed, she got to her feet, with difficulty, since her whole body was weighing her down, then set off for the kitchen at the other end of the corridor. After all, having stayed awake all night, it was quite natural to see to the inner man . . . A milky coffee, some malted milk for the children, that is assuming they had not been put to bed in Henriqueta's room, poor things . . .

Contrary to all her expectations, the door did not open. Dorita decided to ring. It was Saturday, the children must be away in the mountains, as they were every Saturday; Juanjo would be up, so the only person she would be getting out of bed would be Carmina. She wasn't paying her to sleep and she had been ringing the bell for long enough now.

The ringing seeped through the walls, settling on the wall-to-wall carpeting; the time switch clicked and the light went out, plunging her into darkness. A dull fear gnawed at her. What if something had happened? An indistinct noise came from the neighbouring apartment. Hurriedly she put the key in the lock.

The kitchen door was open. She caught a stale smell of disinfectant and cold fat. Carmen switched on the light. The forty-watt bulb left the corners in shadow, but there was no one there.

Perhaps in her bedroom. She gave herself a mental telling-off for not having thought of it before. They had gathered in that simple room, sitting on her narrow bed, prey to the most terrible anxiety.

At the end of the corridor Dorita could see the cold gleam of the massive green-marble dining table Juanjo had ordered directly from Italy. It was so big they were a little cramped for room when standing up, but sitting down they were perfectly comfortable. The bedrooms, impeccably clean and tidy, were open to see as she passed. She gave the kitchen a quick glance, to see what state it was in, then remembered with relief that she had given the maid the day off so she could be alone with Juanjo. Just the two of them together. He must have fallen asleep in the sitting room, poor dear.

Carmen pushed open the door of her bedroom. On the counterpane pulled up over her bed was an envelope. Dumbfounded, she sat down in the chair before picking it up. The tears came to her eyes, the sheet of paper slipped to the floor: 'Carmen, we're not waiting for you. We've gone to stay with Uncle Octavio in his chalet in the mountains. If you're tired, don't bother to come, we'll manage to look after the children without you. There are some fried peppers and meat balls in the fridge. Did you buy my herbal tea? Henriqueta.'

The solid silver frames of the children's first-communion photographs, in place until those of their weddings arrived, glittered in the semidarkness.

'Juanjo . . .'

Her voice faltered. She did an about-turn and headed for their bedroom. The beige silk counterpane reflected the first rays of the sun. She howled.

She pounded the pillow, but to no avail. She stretched out, exhausted, reached for the answerphone and, numb with fatigue and distress, listened to several calls.

'Give me a ring about the *Galerias*, Thursday certainly won't be possible this week. Adela.'

'Mama, send me five thousand pesetas. I'll tell you why.'

She switched it off. The room was beginning to fill with daylight. She decided to sleep for a bit.

A corner of the blanket hit a button on the machine:

'You are connected to the answerphone of the cardiologist, Dr Juanjo Firmin Roquemadas. I am not available at the moment. Please leave your name, address, telephone number and an indication of the reason for your call. I will get back to you as soon as I can. For an appointment, please call my medical secretary on 34 45675. Please speak after the tone.'

Milagrosa – *Mercedes Deambrosis*

'A finely crafted first novel that, in the form of a young woman's childhood recollections of her mother, creates a portrait of the last days of Franco's Spain. Young Maria de los Milagros, known to one and all as Milagrosa, has no one to blame but herself if she's not a child prodigy: after all, her mother Carmen began taking her to school at the age of two. That, admittedly, was more for her mother's benefit than hers – Carmen was the village schoolmistress and saw no reason to waste good money on a babysitter – but it gave Milagrosa something of a head start all the same. A sensitive and sheltered girl, Milagrosa is nevertheless completely overshadowed by her strong and outgoing mother. Used to getting her way, Carmen does not suffer fools gladly: in one of her fits of pique, she even punched out the mayor and was subsequently dismissed from her post. Undeterred, she took a position in her old hometown and moved back with her daughter, sister, and mother (her husband, who refused to move, was unceremoniously left behind). In her new surroundings, during the 1960s, Milagrosa grows up surrounded by all the old certitudes of Spain – making her First Communion; listening to Franco's weekly radio broadcasts – but her coming-of-age is troubled by storm clouds of change looming over Spain and her family alike. Carmen finds herself the victim of a rebellion after her mother dies, when her nephew Arturo stands up to her and demands that his mother receive her fair share (i.e., the greater part) of the estate. That's bad enough, but soon the whole country seems on the verge of turmoil when the elderly Franco falls deathly ill. Can Spain survive without Carmen's beloved caudillo? Can Carmen? The old ways die hard, but hardest of all for the old themselves. An exceptional debut, sensitive and rich without sentimentality.'
Kirkus Reviews

£8.99   ISBN 1 903517 07 9   215p   B. Format

Titles available in the Dedalus Euro Shorts series

Lobster – Guillaume Lecasble
An Afternoon with Rock Hudson – Mercedes
　Deambrosis
On the Run – Martin Prinz